THE WOMAN OWNER-DRIVER

THE COMPLETE GUIDE FOR LADY MOTORISTS

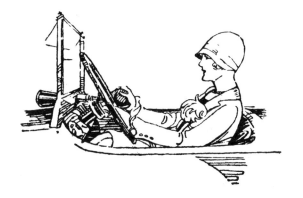

THE HON. MRS VICTOR BRUCE

THE BRITISH LIBRARY

First published in 1928 by Iliffe & Sons Ltd

This edition published in 2014 by
The British Library
96 Euston Road
London NW1 2DB

British Library Cataloguing in Publication Data
A catalogue record for this publication is available from
The British Library

ISBN 978 0 7123 5730 2

Designed and typeset in Perpetua by illuminati, Grosmont
Printed in Hong Kong by Great Wall Printing Co. Ltd

CONTENTS

THE IDEAL MOTORING TEMPERAMENT

RAPIDLY AS the number of women motorists increases, it is but a drop of water to the ocean compared with the number of those who still hesitate to make the plunge. There may be several reasons for that hesitation, but one of the most important, I fancy, is a lurking doubt on the part of the would-be owner-driver of her capacity to control a motor car in the crowded conditions of to-day.

It is not a question of physical strength. The fact that women can drive motor-cars is proved by the fact that women *do*! All kinds of women drive all sorts of cars; and I always think that it is rather a fascinating sight to see a small girl at the wheel of a large car, obviously happy and in perfect sympathy with the vehicle. Providing, therefore, that a woman is in average health, the question of physical ability is one that need not cause a moment's anxiety.

Experts and Others

While it takes all sorts to make the world of motorists there are, it must be confessed, some people whom a hundred years of experience on the road will not transform into really first-class drivers. We cannot all be experts, and there must be degrees in our driving capacity; and I think that though it is the exception for a single individual to possess all the temperamental qualities or characteristics necessary to perfection, the average person, man or woman, is blessed with a sufficient proportion of those characteristics to make a good, sound driver.

The question of the ideal driving temperament, however, is a somewhat controversial subject, though I think that the balance of opinion favours my personal views on the matter. Of the two—the steady, almost stolid, imperturbable individual, and the rather excitable, essentially temperamental driver—I infinitely prefer the latter. He has his off days, it is true; but his general standard is high above the steady mediocrity of the other. And of the several important characteristics which must be present in the ideal driving temperament, he will possess the really vital ones, even though he may be lacking in some respects.

I should say that desirable qualities are six in number:—

1. Imagination.
2. Quick judgment.
3. Determination.
4. Sympathy.
5. Courtesy.
6. Patience.

Numbers 1, 2 and 3 of these characteristics may possibly come into conflict with numbers 4, 5 and 6. But all life's a compromise, and it would be unduly optimistic to expect often to find all six desiderata in one temperament. Further, it is conceivable that in many emergencies on the road the way of safety for all may necessitate an almost brutal exhibition of determination, at the expense of courtesy. However, the variations of the circumstances which may be met with singly or in combination on the road are infinite, and one can but generalise. It may be useful, though, to illustrate with specific instances the application of the various qualities I mentioned above.

1. *Imagination.*—Possession of a lively imagination argues ability to anticipate the probable trend of events from little incidents which a less observant driver might not even notice. It is a deductive, detective ability, and the person possessing it is always prepared for eventualities, as against the succession of shocks which constitute the progress of the unobservant driver. A dog, we will say, is trotting sedately along the

footpath, and is unlikely to cause us any trouble on his own account. But on the other side of the road we see another little dog peeping through a garden gate. Will dog No. 1 see his pal across the way; can dog No. 2 jump through the gap in the gate? Will either make a dash across the road, and, if so, which? It is this kind of triviality which the imaginative mind notices and instinctively thrashes out, with the result that probably gentle acceleration places the car between the two dogs, so that neither can see the other until all possible danger is past. The alternative of the stolid mind is, at worst, the unnecessary murder of somebody's canine friend; otherwise, a swerve endangering human life or, at the best, violent braking may have to be indulged in. Just one other instance: You are following along behind another car in your comfortable saloon, when a violent shower begins. If you are imaginative, you have already noticed, specifically, if unconsciously, that the car ahead is an open two-seater, and the first few drops of rain warn you that the driver in front is likely to pull up, maybe so suddenly that he will forget to give warning, in order to put up the hood.

2. *Quick Judgment.*—The necessity is, of course, self-evident. Perhaps a taxi, in the way that taxis do, swings unexpectedly round a corner in front of you. You have not space, on account of other traffic, to pull out around the taxi, and to use the brakes with the necessary force would be to court a bad skid. Your only course is to follow round the corner—but you have only a fraction of a second to reason all this out and to make the decision.

3. *Determination.*—It is a generally accepted maxim that it is better to insist upon carrying out a decision, even though second thoughts have shown it to be wrong, than to hesitate and reverse that decision. Other drivers may shout at you for doing the wrong thing, but if it is evident that you are determined to carry on with it, they can safely act accordingly. Or, as an illustration of a different kind, supposing you are driving along an open road, and have the right of way, but on the right-hand side is a cart or other obstruction to the progress of an approaching car. The driver of the latter shows symptoms of wanting to steal your right of way. If you give way ever so little, or show any signs of hesitation, quite a nasty situation may arise. Show quite clearly by your handling of the car that you are determined to exercise your right, and all will be plain sailing. In fact, in all circumstances, and in all respects, act decisively.

4. *Sympathy.*—Sympathetic handling of the car is very much more of a matter of temperament than of actual mechanical knowledge. As a negative illustration, let me quote the case of a friend of mine, who did not drive herself. In three successive years, she possessed three cars, each of the highest class and generally regarded as being among the most refined vehicles in the world. Each one she found to be harsh and uncomfortable, especially in the matter of springing, and it was not until I went for a ride with her one day, and severely criticised the driving of her chauffeur that she realised the fault to lie with the driving, and not with the cars. That driver believed that his brakes were for use! He never dreamt of allowing his

speed to drop naturally, but drove hard up to every obstacle in order, apparently, to give a demonstration in four-wheel braking. His cornering, also, was such that the passengers were thrown from side to side, and I found that one had to be constantly braced against the violent oscillation of the car in all directions. Sympathetic driving is not slow driving, just as this harsh handling of the car gives only a semblance of speediness. The sympathetic driver will usually get there first!

5. *Courtesy.*—If you can accomplish a day's run without having given a single soul reason to recall your passage, you have not done so badly! We expect the inevitable anathema from those whom we inconvenience, but there are no medals for decency of behaviour. I think courteous driving rests largely upon an ability to see the other fellow's point of view. How would *you* like to have a klaxon blown in your ear; would *you* appreciate having your best Sunday clothes splashed with mud; would you like to have to push a pram across the tram lines at the double to avoid apparent annihilation of the whole family? Those are the kind of questions which you ought not to have to ask yourself, if that quality of courtesy is your natural possession.

6. *Patience.*—The application in motoring is wide. Reverse the positions in my illustration to No. 3. Do not be too impatient to give the other car the right of way. Do not thrust your way through the crowd of passengers mounting or alighting from a tramcar; and do not force the driver of a heavily laden wagon to pull his horses back on their haunches just because you are too impatient to wait four or five seconds for the wagon to draw clear. Mechanically, too, patience is a valuable attribute.

In starting on a cold morning, allow the engine to warm up before attempting to rev. it, and so avoid burnt valves and seatings; and remember that the oil as well as the water has to be warmed before the engine will function normally and safely.

These are some of the most important points in regard to the motoring temperament; and for the comfort of those members of my sex who are hesitating as to their ability to drive a car, let me say that the average woman has an even better mental equipment than the average man in regard to those peculiar qualities that go to the making of the good driver.

2

THE MOTORING BUDGET

I HAVE SEEN estimates of motoring expenditure so modest as to make one wonder how anyone can contemplate the relative extravagance of travelling by train or bus or of walking; and conversely, I have seen other estimates which appear to make the pastime prohibitively expensive for the majority of people. There must be a happy medium, and I am going to try and work out the average cost of running several different types of cars on the practical basis upon which most of us own and use them.

In the first place I want to emphasise the fact that motoring is a most enjoyable pastime and a convenient means of transport, whether one's means are such that choice is limited to the smallest of two-seaters, or whether the motor house holds a stud of cars. The little car is nowadays so comfortable, lively and efficient, and above all so fully capable of long distance touring that it will afford many owners just the very service they require, quite apart from any question of price or means. Some of the small cars which I have tried recently have been really lovable little things, in the care of which I can imagine any energetic girl taking a keen and enthusiastic interest.

But let us review the question of costs. Before considering the relative expenditures which different types of cars will involve, we will discuss the actual items that have to be reckoned. Petrol, oil, tyres—those are the sources of normal running costs, plus an allowance for minor replacements of such items as lamp bulbs, occasional cleaning when away from home, and small repairs or adjustments which the owner is not competent to effect herself. Unfortunately, however, there are overhead charges which are unaffected by mileage—tax, insurance, garage (when necessary), depreciation, and loss of interest on capital. The last two items are often comfortably ignored in published estimates of costs, partly, I believe, because depreciation is a very difficult subject upon which to lay down hard and fast rules, and partly also because their omission paints the situation in such very much more attractive colours. But I am going to be honest. These items must be considered. If you realise on several hundred pounds' worth of securities in order to buy a motor car, the new investment is not only non-profitable, from a cash point of view, but is actually of dwindling capital value. Supposing you were getting 6 per cent. net on the £300 which your car costs, and that in a year you sell the car for—well, that's the difficulty, because second-hand car values are so variable; but let us say £200. It is perfectly obvious that you must add £118 to the other costs of the year's motoring.

The Question of Depreciation

That particular instance, however, shows us the very blackest aspect of the question. In the first place, a much better figure might have been realised, especially if the car had been chosen originally because it was one of the best sellers in the second-hand market; and in the second place depreciation, so far as price is concerned, is far heavier in a car's first year than it is in succeeding seasons. If we had kept that same £300 car for three years, for instance, we should probably have sold it for very little less than it fetched at the end of twelve months—if we put the figure at £180, the average depreciation per annum comes down with a rush from 33⅓ per cent. to a mere 13⅓ per cent., while the annual cost, including loss of interest, is £58, as compared with the £118 of the other transaction.

I will not go more deeply into the question of depreciation, because it depends upon so many factors which vary in every individual case—the actual interest value of the stock that has to be sold; the purchase price, condition, age and second-hand attractiveness of the car, etc., but I think the folly of being wilfully blind on this question ought to be emphasised.

The cost of keeping and running a motor car varies so widely between the extremes of type that we must take several different grades of vehicle into account, and I propose to tabulate the average costs in regard to the smallest car, the Seven, a medium-powered family type of vehicle, such as a Twelve, and that which most women would consider a big car, of the 18-h.p. or 20-h.p. six-cylinder type. There are several other popular ratings lying between those I have mentioned, but it will not be difficult for those who favour any of them to arrive at the approximate cost of running from an examination of the tables below.

	7.5 h.p. CAR		12.8 h.p. CAR		17.7 h.p. CAR	
PETROL	40 m.p.g.	£17 9 0	25 m.p.g.	£27 18 4	20 m.p.g.	£34 18 0
OIL	1,000 m.p.g.	£3 15 0	1,000 m.p.g.	£3 15 0	1,000 m.p.g.	£3 15 0
TYRES	3 at £2	£6 0 0	3 at £4	£12 0 0	3 at £6	£18 0 0
CASUAL ATTENTION		£3 0 0		£4 0 0		£5 0 0
TAX		£8 0 0		£13 0 0		£18 0 0
INSURANCE		£10 0 0		£12 10 0		£17 0 0
DEPRECIATION (3 years at 15%)	on £150	£22 10 0	on £250	£37 10 0	on £500	£75 0 0
LOSS OF INTEREST at 6%		£9 0 0		£15 0 0		£30 0 0
TOTAL		£79 14 0		£125 13 4		£201 13 0
COST per mile		1.913d.		3.016d.		4.839d.

Petrol, let me say, is taken at the ruling price in London at the time of writing—1s. 4¾d. per gallon; oil at the 5-gallon rate; tyres at an average mileage of 10,000, which is certainly a conservative estimate, given proper treatment; and annual mileage at 10,000 a year. What we really want to arrive at is the cost per mile; but it must be remembered that the greater the distance which is travelled annually, the lower this figure becomes, on account of the inelasticity of the overhead charges. Therefore, if the reader's mileage is likely to be very much more, or very much less, than 10,000, she must make allowance accordingly.

Since these costs are subject to variation in individual cases, and there is always the possibility that a piece of bad luck may necessitate an expenditure that has not been allowed for, it is safer to put the cost per mile in round figures, and say that our little Seven will cost us twopence per mile, our Twelve three-pence farthing, and the larger six-cylinder car fivepence per mile to run. In addition, there may be the question of garage to be provided for, though the majority of houses that are now being erected provide suitable accommodation; while the larger the car, the less likely it is to be washed by the owner herself. Obviously, however, I cannot provide for all these eventualities in a general estimate, and each reader must make the modifications which suit her particular circumstances.

But just consider what you get for your tuppence, three-pence farthing or fivepence a mile! Instant availability of a comfortable means of transport, from door to door; absolute independence of timetables, and accommodation for two, four or five—or even, possibly, seven—people at the given cost per mile. In the case of the smallest car, if we allow three adult passengers, the cost works out at less than half the third class railway fare per person, while even the apparently expensive six-cylinder vehicle will carry its five passengers at only one penny per mile per person!

Rather remarkable, isn't it? I know one can make figures prove anything, but my reckoning is straightforward enough. There is one little point, or rather warning, that I might give to the prospective owner of the Seven, however. The car may only cost you 2*d.* per mile, day in, day out; but you will use it repeatedly for journeys and outings which you would never dream of taking if you had no car. The fact that you can run down to Eastbourne at half the cost of the train fare does not alter the fact that you would not have gone by train. In other words, possession of the car is bound to lead you into what may prove to be little extravagances, and this is a matter which deserves consideration in the settlement of that delicate question of whether or not you can afford to motor.

3

THE IMPORTANCE
OF SUITABILITY

ALL CARS being good in these advanced days, though some
may be better than others, the question of choice depends
almost entirely upon the suitability of the vehicle for the purposes for which it is intended, and very little upon the actual
efficiency of the car itself. In other words, the most ignorant
purchaser cannot go far wrong so long as she limits her selec-
tion to one of the well-known makes. But the question of suitability is so important, so vital to satisfaction, that it should be
given really earnest study before an order is placed. The first
point to be settled is, naturally, the absolute maximum which
one can afford to pay, and the second the amount that can be

placed aside for motoring expenditure per week or month. In the previous chapter I have endeavoured to give a fair estimate of this expense as it applies to three different types of car, and in order to do so I have insisted upon including the item of depreciation. It is worth while remembering, however, that this is not an actual everyday out-of-pocket expense, and in the sense that we are now examining the question it is quite in order to leave the item out of the calculation. The Seven, then, costs less than a pound a week to run, and even in this figure the ultimate necessity to spend a lump sum on new tyres is allowed for. On the same basis, the Twelve will cost roughly thirty shillings, and the largest of the three cars less than two pounds on a 10,000 miles per annum basis.

We have to decide, then, which of those figures we can best afford, with a fairly good margin for unforeseen eventualities, without hardship. Needless to say, while there are average cars at an average price, there are some also which are expensive to buy but economical to run, and others which are just the reverse—cheap to buy and dear to run. The latter might answer very well indeed for the purchaser with a good income but little capital, but it would turn out a hopeless proposition where it was discovered after purchase that the running cost was on an entirely different scale from the distinctly modest first cost.

In deciding, therefore, it is most important that these two aspects of the financial question should be given equal consideration, and while I am on the subject of finance there are two other matters which might be mentioned. The first is the advisability or otherwise of buying a second-hand car.

This has the obvious advantage in most cases of avoiding the terrifically heavy depreciation of the first year, since this is already accounted for in the relatively low price which one pays for the used car. It is worthy of note, also, that the most popular types of vehicle sometimes obtain such high second-hand prices—when it comes to buying them, anyway!—that the saving is barely worth while. One particular make at the moment is unobtainable under about £120 for a current or last year's model, although the price of the new car is only £150. In view of the fact that an engine may have been ruined in its first few miles of life by unsympathetic handling, and that no expert examination will disclose the hidden damage, such a small saving is scarcely worth while.

If, however, it is possible to obtain from a friend who wants to make a change a car of which one really knows the history, and is sure that it has always been well handled and cared for, then there is considerable advantage in the transaction. Also, motor car manufacturers themselves often take in part exchange an old model for one of their latest cars. These exchanges are thoroughly reconditioned, and usually the maker is so satisfied with the efficiency of the car that he issues with it a guarantee, probably for six months. A car of that kind, therefore, is also a safe purchase.

The other matter which I want to discuss is that of hire purchase. I don't know why it is that there is still a reluctance to admit having indulged in the instalment plan of purchase, because it is a perfectly straightforward and often advantageous scheme. Let me put a case. I once heard of a builder who had just completed the development of a large estate and was about to enter on a similar enterprise elsewhere. He was really rolling in money. He had taken one of the houses on the completed estate for his own occupation, and was buying it through a building society, simply because he could make his capital earn a good deal more for him than was represented by the interest which he had to pay on the building society's loan.

It is exactly the same with cars. If you enter into a hire purchase agreement you have to pay a certain interest on the loan, and it is quite likely that your capital is so well invested that the instalment plan will actually save you money. There is also the case of the purchaser with a good income and no capital to speak of. Hire purchase is the only way; but in this case the monthly out-of-pocket expense is naturally very heavy, since the instalments on the car must be added to the running costs. I know this is obvious, but it is surprising how many people have been tempted to an investment which in the course of time proves to be hopelessly beyond their means. Anyway, in every case the question of hire purchase is worthy of consideration, and I do not hesitate to say that the large increase in the popularity of motoring during the past few years is almost entirely due to the improved facilities that are offered for obtaining a car on this system.

Having settled all the financial problems to her individual satisfaction, the reader has probably come to a definite conclusion as to the size and horse-power of the car that will suit her requirements; but she has still to decide between two-seater and four-seater, or between tourer and saloon. A two-seater is an ideal car to drive, and I can imagine circumstances in which the limited accommodation might be an actual advantage.

On the other hand, the owner of a two-seater who almost invariably has the dickey in use would probably be much better satisfied with more commodious coachwork. These are points which each of us must decide for herself. With regard to the question of closed versus open cars, I suppose every motorist of some years' experience has been through the transition stage when, in spite of the growing popularity of the saloon, he or she has fought for that fresh air which we think we love so much! "It isn't motoring, when there's always a roof over your head," or "I like to be able to see the scenery without ricking my neck!" I have said these and similar things myself, but after becoming accustomed to the saloon, most people agree that it is the most suitable car for our climate, and even in our few spells of good weather can be as light and airy, with just as good visibility, as the fully open tourer. For those who use their cars daily for business and general transport as well as week-end or holiday pleasure, there is no question whatever as to the enormously greater advantages of the saloon or coupé; the week-end motorist is in the happy position of being able to please herself, but I do suggest that she makes a point of taking a few long runs in a saloon before deciding against the closed car.

4
METHODS THAT MAKE
FOR EASY STARTING

SINCE I AM WRITING for the average woman owner-driver, and not for the enthusiast who is jealous of any attention given to the car by other hands than her own, I do not feel it necessary to go at all deeply into details of the major matters of car maintenance. It is the exception, I should imagine, rather than the rule, for a girl to undertake the task of decarbonisation, even though she is content to go round the car with a grease gun and the maker's handbook religiously once a week. The handbook will tell her exactly how to take up brake wear, and perform the many little adjustments necessary from time to time; and as the methods employed on different cars vary considerably, there is not much point in my attempting to generalise. In any case, the service offered by the agents of every reputable manufacturer has reached so high a pitch that, taken in conjunction with the standardised schedules of charges for various maintenance jobs, it is scarcely worth while for anyone but a real enthusiast to embark upon tasks that will probably become irksome before they are completed.

There is one little task, however, which every owner must perform for herself; and it is one in which most of us find difficulty at some time or another. This is the starting of the car. A good modern car in sound condition should be, and usually is, instantly responsive to the starter, whether electric or manual; but the best of cars may get out of condition through inexperience or negligence on the part of the owner. The actual fault may be absolutely trivial, but its effect in causing difficult starting is really serious.

Apart altogether from the development of such a fault, the majority of engines require a little humouring in certain circumstances, and I have known several cases among my own friends where a thoroughly good car in perfect condition was rapidly acquiring an unenviable reputation as an obstinate starter simply through lack of knowledge of the owner as to the best way to bring the engine to life. The commonest misconception, and the most prolific source of trouble, is probably the idea that the wider you open the throttle the more gas is drawn in, and consequently the more easily the engine will start! There are plenty of engines which would not start in these conditions if you spun them all day, the reason lying in the design of the carburetter. You must learn the particular idiosyncrasies of your own engine, of course; but, generally speaking, an almost closed throttle concentrates the suction of the engine upon the jet, and draws up a plentiful supply of petrol, while keeping the air orifice small. The result is a strong mixture; a fully open throttle opens wide the air orifice, and, at the low speed at which the engine is turned, reduces the suction on the jet—result, a weak mixture, on which the engine cannot start. An opposite cause—over use of the strangler or choke—may have precisely the same effect. In this case, no air is admitted, and the whole of the suction being concentrated on the only remaining orifice (the bore of the jet) liquid petrol is drawn up and the engine is choked, just as before it was starved.

Save the Starter Motor

Each engine has its own little whims, and it should be one of the first experiments of the new owner to discover, by trial and error, the best combination of settings of the three controls (choke, throttle and ignition) for easy starting. Remember, however, that as the engine should spring into life almost instantaneously, it is quite useless to allow the starter to spin the flywheel for protracted periods. Presuming that the car is new, or otherwise may be supposed to be in sound condition, each attempt to start should not be prolonged beyond a few seconds. If it will not run while you count, say, six, something is wrong—in the case of the starting experiments I have suggested, undoubtedly it is the control settings.

I would like to interpose a remark as to the use of the electric starter, however. When you are deliberately setting out to make a number of starts or attempts to do so, it is obviously much better to use the handle, and so save the batteries. The energy required to turn the engine over is so great that the drain on the battery is something approaching a dead short—and it is a marvel that the modern battery can stand even normal treatment. Be sparing in the use of the starter, therefore.

Care with Coil Ignition

This advice is particularly appropriate in the case of cars with coil and accumulator ignition, since apart from the harm which may be caused to the accumulator by running it right down, there is a point at which insufficient energy is left to actuate the ignition system. The battery will have become too weak to work the starter, of course, but the poor novice labouring at the starting handle will probably not realise that all her efforts are vain, since there is no spark at the sparking plugs! The only remedy when this point is reached is to send to the nearest accumulator service station or garage and have the batteries recharged. It is usually possible to borrow a set that are in good condition in the meantime.

But to revert to our starting problems: I have not said anything about the best position for the ignition lever, but in some cars this also is important. With certain types of magneto the spark becomes weaker as the ignition is retarded, and in spite of the fact that full advance may cause a risk of backfires and a strained wrist or broken arm, it is only in that condition that the engine will start at all readily on a cold morning. This does not apply to coil ignition, for the simple reason that the intensity of the spark is not affected by variation of the firing point. The great thing in such cases is to hold the handle in such a way that the thumb is on the same side as the fingers, since if the engine does take it into its detachable head to run backwards, the handle merely flies out of the operator's hand. With an engine that is at all tricky in this respect, the first effort at starting should always be made with an upward pull, and if it will not start without being really swung round and round, this should be done vigorously, at as rapid a rate of revolutions as can be managed. The faster it is turned, the less is its liability to backfire. Normally, however, a quick snap of the handle past the compression point (which can be judged by the increased resistance) should cause the particular cylinder which is then on its compression stroke to fire at almost the first attempt. That, anyway, is the degree of easy starting at which to aim.

So far I have been dealing merely with the knack of starting an engine in good condition. There are, however, a host of things apart from this which may cause difficulty. Broadly they are all faults of either carburation or ignition, and at a guess I should say that carburation is the more prolific source of trouble. The carburetter itself may be dirty, in which case an almost invisible particle of foreign matter may be obstructing the jet, so that even though the float chamber floods when the needle is lifted off its seating, the necessary vapour cannot reach the engine. This, of course, is easily remediable; and in the case of persistent failure to start it is the first thing, after you have satisfied yourself that the plugs are sparking properly, to be examined. In testing the ignition, by the way, the usual procedure is to detach each wire separately, and to place it in such a position that its end approaches but does not touch some metal portion of the engine. Then when the engine is turned over, either by the starter or by hand, a spark should jump from the end of the wire to the metal. This, it must be realised, is merely a test of the ignition system up to that point, and even though there is a fine fat spark at each of the four, six, eight or twelve wires, it is still possible that the plugs themselves are not functioning properly. The most probable cause of failure then is that in the course of time the actual sparking points, inside the cylinders, have become burnt away sufficiently to increase the gap to such an extent that the spark has not power to jump it at a low rate of engine revolutions. Here is another trap for the novice. She removes each plug from the engine separately, and places it, with its wire attached, with its metal body in contact with the engine. She then turns the engine over—and each plug sparks. What she does not realise is that while the plug may work in the open air, the compressed gas inside the cylinders may offer just that amount of extra resistance which will prove too much for the power of the spark. The obvious course, when the plugs have been removed, is to clean up the points and close the gap slightly—an operation which is nearly always advisable when the engine has been running for a month or so without attention.

And what if the engine still fails to start? Well, if the petrol is reaching the carburetter, the jets are clear, and the plugs are sparking, the trouble is something more serious, though it is quite possible that nothing worse than a loose nut in the carburetter or induction pipe attachment is responsible. This may cause an air leakage sufficient to weaken the mixture drawn into the combustion chamber to a non-startable degree. And, finally, the trouble may be due to an inlet valve which is sticking open, or is not opening at all. Removal of the cover plate over the valve stems, and a close examination of their movements while another person turns the engine over slowly may bring to light the fact that the lock nut on one of the adjustable tappets has loosened, so that the tappet has gradually screwed itself out of adjustment. If anything so simple is found, it is fairly easily put right; and if not, I am afraid that the next step on the track of trouble is the enlistment of professional assistance.

The ignition develops faults so seldom that I have not thought it worth while to suggest a remedy if the tests mentioned above reveal that the trouble lies with the magneto; and, if it does, in nine cases out of ten (and those are the cases for which I am writing) it is much better to let an expert handle the job than to interfere with it one's self.

5

THE GENTLE ART
OF TRAFFIC DRIVING

Traffic driving is not only the novice's bugbear, but is even, so far as London is concerned, somewhat affrighting to many experienced drivers who live in the country, and do not often come to town. I have several friends who will go many miles out of their way rather than cross London in the course of a run, and who will drive no further than the outskirts when they must visit the West End or City, depending thenceforward upon taxis for transport.

As a matter of fact, however, traffic driving is the safest form of motoring there is if a certain few simple rules are followed. The first of these is undoubtedly to keep a watchful eye open for police signals, and to obey them implicitly, and the second is to cultivate a high degree of patience. It is not the slightest bit of use to be in a hurry when your way is obstructed by solid phalanxes of motor buses, and if you do not reconcile yourself to the snail's pace of congested traffic, the resultant irritation is likely to lead to expensive errors of judgment.

But traffic driving falls into several clearly defined categories. There is straightforward travel along a busy thoroughfare; there is the art of leaving the traffic stream for the particular side turning you want; the negotiation of the whirligig which has replaced the confusion that used to exist at most large open spaces where several important roads join; and there is the little problem of parking.

Do as the other traffic does; keep to the general pace, and obey the policemen. That's all there is to straightforward driving; it is when she wishes to leave the traffic stream that the novice often gets into difficulty. In another chapter I have mentioned the necessity for keeping close in to the left-hand side of the road when a left-hand turning is to be taken, and for bearing out to the centre of the road when a right turn is proposed. This is even more important when driving in town, and every time one approaches a main crossing, an effort should be made to take up a position in the traffic consistent with one's future intentions when the "hold up" is released. Usually there will be three or four lines of vehicles abreast, and the presumption is that those on the extreme right wish to take the right-hand arm of the cross roads, those on the extreme left the left-hand arm, and those in the centre are going straight on. Much delay and confusion is caused when this plan is not followed, and the beginner should keep in mind the necessity for taking up her proper position well in advance. While the traffic is still moving it is possible to edge across to right or left, according to which way she wants to turn; but if the manoeuvre is left until the last moment it may prove impossible to cut through the several lines of traffic intervening between the car and its goal.

Round the Circus

Much the same principle applies to the negotiation of gyratory traffic. Before entering the circulating stream, the driver knows whether the turning by which she wishes to leave it is near at hand, or is some distance round the circus. In the former case, she should remain on the extreme outside; in the latter, she should make her way as quickly as possible to the inner ring of vehicles, edging out again gently as she approaches the desired turning. Commonsense and patience in this, as in all other matters pertaining to traffic driving, will soon rob it of its terrors; though the difficulty of finding a suitable place to leave the car while doing the shopping or paying the calls which are the purpose of the trip to town will always remain, I suppose.

When the car is to be left for a few minutes only, it is usually possible to find a convenient side road in which to park; but if you wish to pull up in a main but not very crowded thoroughfare, it is always advisable to ask the nearest constable whether he minds the car being left for whatever the time may be that you expect to be away. If you have chosen your halting place wisely, he will probably be complaisant, while warning you not to be long; if the place is not suitable, the policeman will usually help by suggesting where you may stop. Don't on any account just leave the car and sneak off, hoping for the best. As conditions are in London nowadays, you are almost certain to find the policeman waiting for you on your return.

For a longer stop, there is nothing for it but to find either a garage or a proper parking place; and in regard to the latter I have one or two things to say. Parking places are nearly always crowded during the period of popular meal times; but be sufficiently curious one day to drive right around any car park, and notice the amount of wasted space caused by the untidy parking of quite a number of the cars. If every vehicle had been manoeuvred into position properly, there would have been room for perhaps half a dozen more—yours among them. Instead, the carelessness, lack of proficiency or sheer selfishness of those who have run their cars in anyhow causes you to wander off on a weary, and sometimes vain, search for a vacant place elsewhere.

Where Reversing Counts

The whole art of parking a car tidily and economically, as to the space occupied, is linked up with proficiency in reversing, a subject which should be carefully studied and patiently practised at the outset of the novice's career. There is just one little hint that I might give, however. When you have discovered a space that is large enough, but only just, for your car between the other vehicles, do not attempt to reverse into it at an angle. Drive well out into the road into such a position that you can run straight back into the gap. If you attempt to enter it diagonally, you are almost sure to get into difficulties, and many a scratched and dented wing has been caused by failing to adopt this simple precaution.

Another little point: Before finally parking, notice whether the car alongside which you wish to stop is already jambed up close to the next one beyond it. If it is, and you hem it in on your side also, it may be difficult for the owner to open a door sufficiently widely to enter and drive it away; and while you are away some other thoughtless person may drive up and hem you in also. Even at the expense of using up an extra few inches of parking space, despite what I have already said as to the need for economy in this respect, always make sure that you have left yourself space to open the doors on one side or other of the car.

Sometimes parking is permitted broadside on to the pavement, and that, of course, is the way in which one pulls up outside a shop which it is desired to enter. In this case also some thought should be paid to the task of driving the car out again, and to the avoidance of hemming in the car in front. Always leave a little room in front of you, because anyone who draws up behind your car probably will not! Also, do not stop with the two nearside wheels actually rubbing against the kerb. Apart from the damage caused in this way to the tyres, you will find it extremely difficult to draw away from the kerb in the small amount of space available, and will probably have to wait until the owner of the car ahead or at the rear returns before you can drive off.

Damage to the tyres may equally be caused by reversing back to the kerb, in the case of the more usual method of parking. In a bad case, the tube may be seriously nipped, while you may also be committing a breach of the local parking regulations, by letting your luggage carrier or rear trunk project over the footpath.

The Tramcar Problem

An aspect of traffic driving which I have not mentioned is that of one's behaviour on the tram lines. It ought not to be necessary at this late date—though I am afraid it is—to say that the motorist should never force her way through the crowd mounting or descending from a stationary tram car. This is, in fact, an offence in many Continental and some British towns, and is, anyway, one of the worst forms of inconsiderate driving. From the point of view of personal safety, trams should be given a wide margin, on account of their remarkable braking powers; and for the good of the tyres and the avoidance of skidding, every effort should be made to keep out of the tramlines. Cars vary considerably in the degree of difficulty of turning the wheels out of the lines; with some, one may be dangerously trapped. In regard to the overtaking of tramcars, the law varies in different places. In London, they may be overtaken on either side, whereas in Glasgow and other cities at home and abroad it is forbidden to overtake on the offside. And this reminds me of another dangerous trap for which tramlines are responsible. Sometimes without warning the lines swerve in towards the nearside kerb, and unless the driver is wary she may find herself running into a closing gap which is obviously not wide enough to allow the passing of the car. In such cases the conductor of the car, if he is not busy collecting fares, will usually hold up a warning hand, but in this, as in all other matters connected with the driving of a motor car in traffic or in the country, the safest way is to depend upon one's own observation.

6

"PHYSICAL JERKS" AND HOW TO AVOID THEM!

THERE ARE so many things that the would-be car driver must learn to do, and not to do, that I am not quite sure which is the easier task—either for the learner, or for me in endeavouring to describe the most important points in each category. At the moment, let us consider some of the worst of what must be regarded as bad driving habits. I think quite *the* worst and a fault that is growing still more common, is unnecessary, and often misleading, hand signalling.

There are few occasions when it should be necessary to signal, providing that one is driving properly, but it is vital that any signals that are given should be clear and open to no misunderstanding.

There are four or five signals in common use, and I want to examine them individually, with a view to substantiating my statement that their use can generally be omitted if the car is driven correctly.

1. *I am slowing down*. The arm is extended with the palm of the hand downwards, the hand being waved up and down.
2. *I am going to stop*. The arm is raised vertically from the elbow, palm forwards.
3. *I am turning to the right*. The arm is extended horizontally, palm forwards.
4. *I am turning to the left*. The arm is extended horizontally, and waved from rear to front, indicating that traffic may overtake.
5. *You may overtake me*. Same signal as No. 4, given in reply to the horn signal of a car behind, the driver of which wishes to pass.

Well those are the signals, and it is wise for the beginner to learn the different actions so that when the necessity arises she can give them accurately. In a few moments I will describe some of the errors which are committed in signalling; but in the meantime I have to justify my own words as to the frequent lack of necessity for any signal at all.

Generally speaking, then, in town traffic the driver has all her work cut out to look after the control of her own car, and to keep a wary eye on the car in front; and in the country every material alteration of direction or speed should be so gradually performed that the intentions of the driver are clearly indicated by the movements of the car. A sudden necessity to slow down in either town or country leaves no time for signalling; and the inherent weakness of the matter is that, owing to the slipshod methods in use, you cannot be sure (*a*) that the signal of another driver really means what it appears to indicate, or (*b*) that, in the absence of a signal, no deflection or change of pace will occur.

Signal No. 1. Now I think I have shown that this should not be necessary, because slowing down should never be performed so suddenly that other drivers can be taken by surprise; and when, as in traffic, the necessity does arise other drivers are already awake to the possibility. Frequently such emergencies arise only through following along too closely behind another vehicle. In this case, not only is the general trend of the traffic obscured from view, but the driver leaves herself little or no safety margin. If the car in front does slow up suddenly, she may have found the value of buffer bars before she has time to apply her own brakes. Incidentally, that safety margin is rather critical, depending largely on the speed at which the traffic is moving. If too great a gap is left, taxis or other cars will probably nip in at the first opportunity, so that the happy medium—a space which gives one time for action, and allows some sort of a view of other traffic besides the vehicle immediately in front, and yet is not sufficiently great to afford an obvious temptation to inconsiderate drivers to cut in—should be aimed at.

Signal No. 2. This is usually necessary in traffic or on a crowded road, but even then the car will have been pulled in gradually to the kerb or side of the road, and the driver should in any case satisfy herself that there is no other vehicle following immediately behind before she actually applies the brakes with the intention of stopping. Thus, in the ordinary circumstances of motoring, the gentle diminution of speed, plus the pulling in to the near side, has already warned other drivers that a stop is intended.

Signal No. 3. Since a turn to the right involves cutting across the line of traffic in the opposite direction, considerable slowing down is necessary, quite apart from the safe speed at which the actual corner can be taken. According to traffic conditions, the car is edged gently out towards the middle of the road, and while this manoeuvre should prepare following traffic for the coming turn, it is advisable also to indicate definitely, with a well-extended arm, that a turn to the right is projected.

Signal No. 4. The preliminary actions of the driver, in pulling in to the extreme left-hand side of the road before a left-hand turning are the same as those which would precede an actual halt, and as the corner is usually more blind, owing to the method of its approach, considerable reduction of speed is necessary. Before the corner is reached, therefore, other traffic is automatically overtaking on your off side, in normal fashion.

Signal No. 5. An overtaking driver does not sound his horn to ask if he may pass, but to signify his intention of doing so. On a wide road, he merely asks you not to meander across to the wrong side, and not to wobble for a moment or so. On a narrow road, he asks you to squeeze in as far to the left as you conveniently can. There is no need to signal permission to overtake; you will want both hands to hold your car straight, and to give as much space to the overtaking driver as courtesy demands and safety permits. Your immediate action in pulling in to the left tells him that you are prepared, and in a flash he is gone.

In regard to the slipshodness with which signalling is often performed, I think the worst fault is that of the driver who drapes his—or her, mind you!—arm down the side of the car in such a position that the signal cannot possibly be seen.

In the case of the beginner, I fancy that lack of proficiency in the mechanical control of the car makes her fear to take her eyes off the road ahead for a single instant, with the result that she never throws a glance behind, or into the driving mirror. Obviously, however, such a glance will show whether the road behind is clear, or whether a moment's patience is necessary before pulling up or taking a side turning.

7

MORE BAD DRIVING HABITS TO BE AVOIDED

Bad driving habits, with which, in the previous chapter, I have dealt only in so far as they concern hand signalling, are many and various. It is, for instance, particularly bad to forget, or ignore, the ignition lever and to allow the engine to reach that stage of labouring which is indicated by "knocking." After a very little experience, the driver knows that in certain circumstances the engine *will* knock; and knows that the knocking can be stopped by a slight movement of the ignition lever. Why, therefore, allow the knocking stage to be reached at all? The answer is, of course, obvious: Because the beginner does not realize that it is distinctly injurious to the engine to allow it to labour in this way.

Ignition Control

The ideal method of driving would be to keep the ignition advance always, in all changes of load and gradient, just short of the degree which would cause knocking, but in practice it is not necessary to exercise quite so critical a control. It should be borne in mind, however, that it is very nearly as bad a habit to run continually with the ignition too much retarded as too far advanced, since this causes loss of power, excessive petrol consumption, and other more serious ills, such as pitting of the valve faces and seatings.

Another inexcusable habit is to make use of a slipping clutch to avoid gear changing, towards the top of a long hill, or in moving away from a traffic halt. This is a deliberate sin of commission; but the same fault is committed in ignorance or accident in the course of changing gear itself. There are many modern cars with which the clutch must not be slipped at all; others which are not quite so delicate in this respect. But in any case, it should be remembered that the clutch is simply an apparatus by means of which the engine can be disconnected from the transmission, and allowed to take up the drive again with a certain amount of elasticity. It is not intended to be slipped more than sufficiently to provide a shockless take-up of the drive, and since this depends upon the adhesion of two spring loaded friction surfaces, it is obvious that *any* slipping between these surfaces must cause wear. Even the brakes, which act on the same principle, need relining in the course of time, and they are designed for the job! Letting in the clutch should in all circumstances be a definite and deliberate action, undue shock being avoided as far as possible by regulating the rate of engine revolution so that it agrees with the road speed of the car, according to the particular gear which is in use. This may sound a rather expert matter, but really it only calls for a little thought and intelligent practice.

A bad habit which a little thought should cure is that of sounding the horn either too soon or too late. In the first case, you hoot away merrily at a car in front which you wish to overtake, and say all sorts of rude things about the driver who will not give way. Actually he hasn't heard your signals at all; in fact, it is not much use hooting until you are right behind the car, unless the horn with which your car is fitted is particularly raucous or penetrating. Belated hooting, on the other hand, may easily cause an accident. I am thinking more of occasions when it is necessary to warn pedestrians or cyclists. If they have not heard you coming, and you give a blast of the horn almost in their ears, it is impossible to depend on their actions in the momentary fright which you have caused them. As a matter of fact, there are many such occasions when silence is golden. If a pedestrian is ambling across the road, and is oblivious of your presence, you can usually tell whether there is any possible chance of his altering his mind in mid stream. If there is not, it is far better to let him go on in ignorance and safety than to chance the fact that he may start at the note of your horn, and step back into the path of the car.

I am afraid that a whole volume might be written on misuse of the brakes; but beyond saying that you should drive always with a view to avoiding the use of the brakes as much as possible, and that the better you are able to drive, the fewer will be the occasions when it is necessary to apply them with violence, I will not go into detail. There is one aspect of the question, however, which should be mentioned, and that is braking in connection with cornering. The inexpert way is to misjudge speed slightly in approaching a corner, and then to check the car with the brakes while rounding it. This is quite wrong, and may easily be fatal if the car's speed is much too high, or the road is greasy. It is, of course, largely a matter of the judgment which only experience will give; but the way to take a corner with the least possible loss of speed is to check the car with the brakes before the bend is reached, and actually to accelerate while the car is on the corner. It will probably astonish the novice to find that acceleration definitely assists the steering, and holds the car on its course, whereas braking in the same circumstances tends to throw the tail outwards and makes the steering heavy.

Cutting in, a term which I suppose every one now understands, is so obvious a fault that I don't think I need worry about it. Other bad habits are possible in connection with overtaking, however. One is that of pulling out a good deal farther than is actually necessary for safety in passing another car; another is that of making a third line of traffic by passing two cars at once, or by overtaking when another vehicle is coming in the opposite direction. There are times, perhaps, when the action is justifiable, but as a golden rule for novices I should say "Don't!" Time will bring proficiency; knowledge of exactly what acceleration the car possesses, and ability to drop into a lower gear to improve the acceleration so that the car can be positively jumped out of an awkward predicament; but until such time the novice should be ultra cautious in this matter of overtaking. I have often seen what the driver imagines to be caution carried to too great lengths, however. The car which he wishes to overtake is going, apparently, at only a very few miles an hour less than he wishes to travel himself. He pulls out and overtakes, but without the least increase above his normal speed, with the result that the process of overtaking and drawing sufficiently ahead to be able to pull in to the left without cutting in on the overtaken car occupies an appreciable space of time. All the while there is another car, unsuspected but impatient to get on, behind. Whether the driver's impatience is justified is beside the point, which is that when overtaking your principal thought should be to complete the manoeuvre and cease to be a possible hindrance to other traffic as quickly as possible.

Following closely behind a tram is a particularly dangerous habit, as the best of our modern four-wheel brakes do not approach the retarding power of the electric vehicle when the driver chooses to, or must, use it; while another bad habit easily acquired, is that of ignoring road signs, in one's interest in either the scenery or in conversation with one's passenger.

And I have no doubt that there are plenty of others, though the bad habits I have mentioned are some of the worst.

8

SOME LITTLE POINTS
OF LAW AND INSURANCE

THE FORMALITIES to be complied with when the car is ready for delivery are few and simple, and as, in any case, they are usually performed for the purchaser by the agent from whom she buys the vehicle, there is no need for me to go very deeply into the ordinary legal details affecting motoring. Unfortunately, however, the most careful and considerate driver in the world may come into contact with the law at some period or periods in her motoring career, and there are several little points upon which I am, from sorrowful experience, able to give a few hints.

The ordinary formalities consist merely of registering the car and obtaining its index letters and numbers, a process which involves payment of the licence duty for the year, or such part of the year as is appropriate, and the taking out of a driving licence. Apart from this, however, I prefer to regard the insurance of vehicle and driver against all eventualities as a duty also.

No Excuse for Recklessness

Needless to say, the possession of an insurance policy does not justify one in taking the slightest risk; in fact, although the company's payment of a claim does not depend upon the lack of culpability of its client, it is quite possible that a renewal of the policy may be refused. And if one company thus refuses to accept a risk on account of proven negligence or recklessness in a previous accident, it will be difficult, if it is not impossible, for the person concerned to find any other insurance company which will accept her. This may not matter at the moment, since at the time of writing third party insurance has not yet been made compulsory; but I do not think there is much doubt that some such provision will be a part of future legislation. Then driving an uninsured car will be as serious a misdemeanour as continuing to drive with a suspended or cancelled licence.

There is another little point in regard to insurance which is probably not known to a great many people. A car owner who would never dream of taking her car on the road at all without full insurance, is liable to be casual concerning the renewal of her driving licence. If she is caught in the few days which may elapse between the expiry of the old licence and its renewal, the worst that can happen, she thinks, is a more or less negligible fine. If she reads her insurance policy, however, she will find that the cover against risk often applies specifically to a *licensed* driver. In carrying on with an out-of-date licence, therefore, she risks not only the fine, but a claim, in the case of an accident, for damage which may involve financial ruin. I will say nothing of the morality of the question of risking injury to persons or damage to property without the means of affording compensation; and if, and when, compulsory insurance becomes an item of motoring law, the results to the motorist will be even more serious than they are now.

Silence is Golden

In the case of an accident, or of any kind of clash with the police, silence was never more golden. Say no more than is inevitable; and on no account enter into an argument as to whose action caused the accident. The question of personal injury apart, your sole purpose should be to secure the names and addresses of witnesses. The last thing you want is a public debate. As to the police, the less said the better. Remarks made in the heat of the moment, in sarcasm, or in alleged wit will not sound the same when reproduced from the policeman's notebooks in the ultimate court proceedings. They will not serve to improve matters for you, and will most likely merely increase the amount of the fine.

Reverting to accidents, naturally you would never make an admission of fault; but sometimes the action of the driver of a car in front necessitates a move on your part which involves a third car in a collision with your own. It is very natural, but very unwise, to excuse yourself by blaming someone else. This is a tacit admission of fault, since in law, as in other affairs of life, two wrongs do not make a right. The argument is that you should always be prepared for the erratic behaviour of other people, and although the same argument applies to the driver of the third vehicle, who should have been ready for your sudden swerve or halt, it doesn't let you out!

Never overtake another motor vehicle in a ten-mile speed limit, nor in a village if it can possibly be avoided. Traps are still laid for the impatient, and the mere fact of speeding up momentarily to pass even a tradesman's decrepit van will bring up your average speed to a point above the little latitude allowed, if there is a police trap. And if there is not, the zealous local constable may derive a totally erroneous impression of your intentions if you overtake anything at all. Dangerous driving is an unpleasant charge to meet, as well as a difficult one to dispel.

Politeness Pays

And remember, courtesy always pays in one's dealings with the police. Apart altogether from policy, the treatment which the motorist sometimes has cause to bemoan is not the fault of the policeman himself. He is only obeying orders, and the fact that your car is the one which he happens to have timed is merely your bad luck. As I said before, you cannot improve matters by venting your displeasure upon him.

The policeman's life, in any case, is not a particularly easy one, especially if he is on point duty at a busy road junction, and the least you can do is to follow his directions implicitly. Don't run past his hand; and if you do, through a spasm of mental aberration, don't throw the blame on to his confusing signals. Apologize for your own stupidity, and he will probably say: "Oh, go on: I can't stop to argue!" A certain amount of tact is a very valuable attribute.

9

COMFORT AND EFFICIENCY IN MOTORING CLOTHES

MOTORING CLOTHES have gone the way of the crinoline and bishop sleeves. It is no longer necessary or smart to wear special garments in the car, for the simple style of everyday frocks, coats and hats is almost ideal for motoring purposes. One would be almost justified in arguing, in fact, that fashion has been actually influenced by the special requirements, in the matter of women's clothes, of the ever more popular motor car. It is probably nothing but a coincidence, however; but the fact remains that no matter what the daytime function may be to which one is proceeding, in dressing for the part, one is also suitably clad for motoring.

Suitable Footwear

But because we no longer need to keep a special motoring wardrobe, there is no need to go to the other extreme, and neglect a few obvious precautions which will benefit our personal comfort, our pockets, or our appearance. I think perhaps I might begin on the subject of shoes, for I must confess that the usual thin-soled, smart walking shoe is scarcely suitable for driving, for more than one reason. The beginner will no doubt learn from experience, but I expect she will be very much surprised to find that constant use of the car effects no economy in shoe leather! There is quite considerable wear through the use of the pedals, and this is particularly true of the right foot, which is always in contact with the accelerator or brake pedals. With some cars—perhaps the majority— the usual position of the feet of the driver causes rapid wear at the back of the heels, while in addition an unsubstantial shoe quickly becomes more or less shapeless. Apart from this, however, a very light shoe is unsuitable in that it does not give proper control of the car, and is consequently both unsafe and fatiguing. It is a simple matter to set aside a special pair of brogues, or anything comfortable and substantial, to be worn while one is actually driving, and to have with one a smart pair into which to change when there is any walking to be done where appearance is important. Practically everything I have said as to shoes applies equally to gloves, for the comfortable, and even baggy, gloves which are desirable for driving purposes are scarcely suitable for wear when one is separated from the car. Again, it is easy to change.

The modern light-tinted stockings are something of a problem, too, since they cannot so readily be changed on the car! The slightest spot of oil or grime destroys the immaculateness on which they depend for their effect—and no matter how careful one may be there is almost bound to be some dirt in the neighbourhood of the pedals and levers. A plan that I have found effective is to wear one of the several kinds of woolly gaiters or spattees, partly for the sake of warmth, and partly for the protection of light stockings.

And now we come to the more serious if not more important question of hats and coats. With a saloon car, nothing unusual in the way of a coat is necessary, unless it be for really long-distance driving in winter time. Then I have found the most effective as well as the most comfortable garment to be one of the various skin coats which are wind proof and warm without being heavy. But it must be a short coat, since otherwise the skirts simply will not stay put, and keep one in a constant state of fidgets that entirely destroys the pleasure of the run. In very cold weather in an open car it is important to wear a belt, even with such a coat as I have mentioned, in order to prevent the cold air from blowing up inside and chilling one's back. Most people say that if the feet are warm, the whole body keeps warm, and while this is mostly true, there is nothing more likely to be productive of a serious illness than that chilliness which results from allowing the wind to penetrate beneath the protective covering of the coat.

In summertime, however, these precautions are unnecessary, for even on an open touring car the majority of people keep the side screens in place throughout the year, and the full effect of the wind is never felt. In regard to protection from dust of dainty frocks, the saloon with its windows wide open is little better than an open car; some sort of dust coat, therefore, should be worn. If a very light fabric is chosen this is apt to be a nuisance, but I have found that a fairly heavy linen is suitable for the purpose, without fluttering in the breeze too much. A hook and eye or other fastening an inch or so below the knees is useful in keeping the necessarily long skirts in place.

Hats and Headaches

Most of the tight-fitting hats of to-day are quite suitable for motoring, but there is one little point to guard against, and that is too tight a fitting. It is bad for the hair, makes it greasy, and quickly removes the cherished wave, and if worn for long hours at the wheel causes bad headaches. The lack of ventilation is no doubt the cause of the ill-effect upon the hair itself, and I have come to the conclusion that the best headgear for summer wear, more particularly in a closed car, when the sun cannot beat down directly on the head, is a sports net, with a dark shaded peak to protect the eyes. That, by the way, is another important point in regard to the motoring hat. Whatever its shape, it must shield the eyes from the evening sun, either with a permanently turned down brim, or with one which can be pulled down when the occasion arises.

Fortunately there is no need to warn the reader against anything elaborate and fluttery in the way of hats or clothing generally, though I might mention that a loose scarf, whether worn by the driver or the passenger by her side, should be avoided. At a critical moment it may catch the wind and blow across the driver's vision, with, possibly, tragic results. Frocks themselves are almost severely simple, but in the matter of jewellery fashion does allow us to express a little individuality. But not on the car! Even so simple an adornment as a string of pearls is better either not worn or safely tucked out of the way, as it is very liable to become entangled in the control levers on the steering wheel. I do not care about wearing anything but the most simple of rings, as, apart from the fact that they may interfere in the control of the car, it is difficult to avoid chipping the stones through an accidental knock on the gear or brake lever.

And now I want to say a word about the car itself which has a very important if indirect bearing on the question of clothes. Quite the best scheme I know for the protection of dainty frocks is the use of loose covers for the seats. Good substantial leather upholstery does not itself need protection, you may say. No; but it is invariably dark in colour, and the casual smudge of oily dirt which a garage hand—in both senses—has left as a mark of appreciation does not show, until you have sat upon it! That smudge does show on a light coloured loose cover, and you can avoid it. The cover will need cleaning; but the frock would have been ruined. If the upholstery is of Bedford cord or similar material, the need for loose covers is all the more apparent, and I think it will be agreed that the extra cost of the covers soon justifies itself, especially when it is remembered that the careful protection of the upholstery will bring its reward in an enhanced selling value when you feel you want to make a change.

PRACTICAL POINTS
ON PICNICKING

HOTEL ACCOMMODATION in the majority of districts visited by cars being inadequate for our motoring millions, and the means of those millions often being inadequate to meet hotel charges as a regular thing, the question of picnicking and camping out may be regarded from a practical as well as a romantic standpoint.

On the latter ground alone, however, in the majority of cases the freedom of a picnic meal in chosen surroundings adds to the pleasure of a motor jaunt, whereas the delay and expense attached to a restaurant or hotel meal are regarded at best as necessary evils. In fairness to hotel keepers, I must admit that there has been a noticeable improvement in the quality and the variety of the fare provided in recent years, no doubt on account of the fact that with the rapid increase in motoring the problem of catering is becoming simplified.

We need not inquire further as to why picnicking is and should be popular. It is; so let's consider how to make it most satisfying and enjoyable. Well, first of all, I consider money well spent on a properly fitted picnic basket, especially as a serviceable article can now be obtained at a really reasonable price. Apart from the fact that the scientifically designed containers in such a basket keep food and liquid in better condition, it is more pleasant in every way to avoid the numerous loose parcels and bottles which are a feature of the badly organised picnic.

A spirit stove and a kettle are essential items in the equipment, and if the stove is one of the kind which burns petrol, the problem of fuel and how to carry it is automatically solved. An incidental advantage is that these stoves are not rendered ineffective in a breeze, whereas with the type using methylated spirit it is difficult to shield the flame, and tea preparation is often a lengthy and troublesome business.

Some people will continue to pin their faith to the thermos flask, but the elimination of the task of tea making does not, to my mind, compensate for the fact that the beverage is never so good as when freshly made; some advantage is gained, however, by putting the tea only into the flask, and adding milk at the moment when it is desired to drink the tea.

But I will not go into details as to the kind of food most suitable for picnicking, since tastes vary widely. Neither will I do more than refer to the desecration of the countryside caused by the debris of picnics. There is always, apparently, more rubbish left over than the amount of material with which we start the meal, and its disposal is often rather a problem. Sometimes one may bury tins and burn paper; but to carry the rubbish away from the scene of the picnic and throw it in some convenient ditch is distinctly not a solution. I long ago reconciled myself to the necessity, if no suitable rubbish dump came to light in the course of the return journey, of carrying the tins and wrappings all the way home and depositing them in the domestic dustbin!

Precautions Necessary and Advisable

The need for precaution against firing the gorse or bracken amid which one takes a meal is another matter which needs only passing reference; and I think the desirability, if milk or tinned provisions are carried loose in the car, of keeping them away from the heat of the engine is equally obvious.

A point which, according to my observation, does not occur to many people is that while they are choosing a shady spot for themselves, the car is left out in the blazing sun without protection of any kind. In really hot weather a good deal of damage can be done in this way, for exposure to the steady heat, without the mitigating draught of air which keeps the surfaces cool during actual travel is good for neither paint-work, upholstery nor tyres. Unfortunately this is a precaution which in this country need not often worry us. Rather do we have to provide against the ill effects of sitting on damp ground, and an essential part of the picnicking equipment is a rubber ground sheet, on which rugs and cushions may be spread. When the ground is at all soft, also, care is required in the placing of the car so that when the time comes to start, its rear wheels will not spin and dig themselves in.

Parking for the Picnic

There are increasingly few places these days where it is reasonable to leave the vehicle on the public highway, since a single stationary car can cause widespread obstruction to other traffic, but it is usually possible to pull off the road in such a fashion either that the rear wheels themselves remain on hard ground, or that there is a slight slope which, when the brake is taken off, will itself allow the car to drop back on to terra firma without the use of the engine. If through bad judgment when reversing back to the road, the wheels do begin to spin, the clutch should be withdrawn instantly, because the longer the spinning is allowed to continue the worse the situation becomes. The united efforts of the picnic party, plus very cautious and gentle use of the engine will usually induce the car to move away if the ground is only moderately soft—though sometimes it may be necessary to lay a hard track of such stones and brushwood as may be obtainable. The great point is that once the car is on the move it must be kept moving. If the wheels cease to revolve for an instant, the spinning will begin again. But wise choice of location on a slope will invariably avoid all this trouble.

For those who want to go even further on the road to complete independence, camping out offers delightful possibilities of pleasure and economy. Actual caravanning, possibly, does not appeal to everyone. I think myself that it is an acquired taste, while the cost of either purchasing or hiring a caravan trailer, the difficulty of storing it, if purchased, when it is not in use, and fear that the car may be difficult to manage with its trailing encumbrance will probably act as deterrents so far as the majority of motorists is concerned.

I have discovered—although I suppose there is nothing new in motoring—an effective compromise, however, which is inexpensive and convenient, and serves excellently for those who wish for only an occasional night or so of camping. It depends upon whether the front seat or seats of the car are removable; if they are, an air mattress may be made to fit the floor space, and by removing the rear cushion and replacing with a pillow, a comfortable bed may be made up. When not in use and deflated, the air mattress rolls or folds up into a comparatively small space, and is, of course, easily put into commission again when required.

If further accommodation is required, tents of the lean-to variety, using the car as one of the walls, are inexpensive to purchase, or even quite simple to make, and they also take up little luggage space, while the commissariat is attended to by the picnic basket which I think ought to be a permanent item in the equipment of every car.

Talking about luggage reminds me that it is unwise to load up with a lot of junk, the use of which is problematical, especially when setting out on a fairly ambitious tour. Wireless sets and gramophones and similar impedimenta may be justifiable for a day's outing or even a week-end trip, but the less luggage that is not absolutely essential one carries on a tour the better. The essentials are difficult enough to pack, and if excessive use is made of the rear luggage carrier, the handling and even the safety of the car may be seriously affected.

THE IDEAL SUMMER HOLIDAY

I THINK ONE of the principal attractions of the motor car must be the wonderful advantages it confers in the matter of summer holidays. Gone are all the miseries of catching trains, sweltering in overcrowded carriages, getting into and out of cabs and antiquated seaside "flies"; and gone, likewise, the worries of shepherding one's little flock through the various transport changes incidental to the old-fashioned annual visit to the coast. Instead, with a very vague and general idea of destination, one sets off into the blue, finding interest, novelty, health and even instruction every inch of the way.

Delightful Uncertainty

Different people's ideas vary as to the best method of conducting a touring holiday, of course; but personally I think that a great part of its charm, apart from the independence of the motorist, is its delightful uncertainty. There is really no need to make for a definite town each night, in England, anyway. A pretty old world village at the end of late afternoon is a very much more desirable resting place than the big town, twenty miles or so away, to reach which may involve another hour or so of travelling, perhaps on strange roads through the gathering dusk, when the party is already tired with the excitements of a long day on the road. Should that fascinating, rose-covered inn prove to be a popular angling hostelry, with no accommodation to spare, well, we can still go on—but it is this uncertainty and lack of cast iron schedule that is so delightful to me.

A certain amount of planning is necessary, naturally, and particularly in regard to luggage and the equipment of the picnic basket, with which I have dealt in the previous chapter. In course of time one becomes expert in plotting out, and accomplishing, a tour on the particular lines which best suits the taste of the party. In other words, while the sheer joy of that first tour can never be fully recaptured, it is possible that it may have fallen somewhat short of perfection through various little errors and omissions of organisation which are so easily avoided—when one knows!

Probably the greatest error of the majority of people is to attempt to do too much. The motor car is so convenient and tireless a means of transport that the enthusiastic beginner is apt to forget that human beings have their limits of endurance even though the car has not, with the result that each day is concluded in a state of utter fatigue. It is rather unfortunate that since we usually choose a touring ground a few hundred miles away from home, and since the roads leading thereto have lost their novelty through repeated day and week-end journeys, there is a temptation to pile up the mileage on the first day or so in order to reach the actual touring district as quickly as possible. I do not think I am exaggerating in saying that this is almost fatal to real enjoyment.

Touring needs a certain amount of preparation for the majority of motorists, who spend their town lives more or less indoors. Sitting still for long hours on end alone is tiring; the accommodation of the body to the movement of the car, unconscious though it may be, is astonishingly vigorous exercise; exposure to the strong, unaccustomed air of the country takes its toll of physical endurance; and, above all, the mental activity needed to take in and appreciate the constantly moving panorama is extremely tiring until one gets used to it. It can be imagined, therefore, what is the effect of covering two hundred or more miles on each of the first few days; and the initial extremity of fatigue may well take so long to live down that the greater part of the tour is spoiled. The actual distance to be covered per day, however, is very largely a matter of circumstance. On a wide, smooth main road on which there is nothing of interest to cause repeated stops for sight seeing, and with a fast, smooth-running, easily driven car, two hundred and fifty miles may not seem over long; whereas in circumstances the exact reverse of those which I have outlined it is extremely probable that a total mileage of one hundred may strike the voyagers as a good day's work. I will not be didactic on the matter of daily mileage, therefore; but I do say: Do not overdo it!

The matter of luggage, also, alone can make or mar a holiday. Although most cars nowadays are fitted with rear luggage grids, to be perfectly honest it must be admitted that a four-seater car does not provide unlimited luggage accommodation for its complement of passengers, especially if picnic equipment, cameras and an assortment of coats and walking sticks (not to mention golfing and fishing implements) have to be carried as well. So far as the car itself is concerned, therefore, pretty vigorous use of the economy axe is required in the matter of each passenger's personal luggage. One suit case per passenger is the utmost that I will allow; and although this has sometimes necessitated an emergency purchase in some town *en route* neither I nor my passengers have ever found ourselves seriously inconvenienced in even our most ambitious tours.

Luggage by Rail

It is possible, of course, even on a strictly non-schedule tour, to pick out on the map a town here and there at which one determines to stop at some time or other; and any luggage which simply must be taken but cannot be accommodated on the car can well be sent on in advance. Exchanges of clean for soiled garments and so forth can then be made, and the trunk sent off home again. A little thought on this subject will save no end of inconvenience and trouble on the journey. Nothing is worse, I think, than to have to do a lot of useless packing and unpacking each day, and left to ourselves, even the most methodical of us will take a number of garments and articles which *might* be of use—but never are! It is amazing, in fact, to discover at the stern urge of necessity, how few of the things which the average traveller takes are really indispensable.

Well, as you see, I believe in travelling light, and not solely on account of the trouble that is thus avoided in regard to repacking each morning. Overloading of the car is undoubtedly one of the principal things that must be guarded against on a tour, because an overflow of bags and packages from the luggage carrier to the interior, of the car means less comfort for the passengers—and in the course of a long day's run being unable to shift one's position just exactly how and when one will becomes most irritating and irksome. The car itself deserves consideration, and in this respect overloading of the luggage carrier has seriously bad effects. That carrier, it should be remembered, usually projects considerably behind the rear axle, and the greater the dead weight carried there the worse will it be both for car and driver. Steering is immediately affected, and the car may even be dangerously unstable on a greasy surface. The ideal form of rear luggage accommodation is the trunk which is supplied as part of the standard equipment of so many modern cars, especially of the fabric bodied variety. Besides doing away with the necessity for carrying two fairly heavy suitcases, this is built so that it nestles closely into the contour of the car, and thus the undesirable overhang beyond the rear axle is reduced.

As to general advice on motor touring I should say that it is always advisable to call it a day fairly early in the evening, before anyone of the party has really begun to feel tired. Dinner then becomes an enjoyable meal, instead of a duty—often neglected by the over-fatigued traveller, who has no thought beyond bed!—and the events of the day or the plans for the morrow can be pleasantly talked over. If for any reason it is necessary or desirable on any particular day to cover an abnormal mileage, it is far better to make the little effort required for an unusually early start. The back of the journey is then broken before luncheon, and that which remains can be taken just as suits the party, without the usual rush at the end of a long run to avoid travelling in strange country through too many hours of darkness.

1 2

PICTURE MAKING ON TOUR

WHATEVER I may have said in other chapters regarding the avoidance of overloading, and of carrying useless impedimenta, must not be taken to include cameras. No tour is complete without at least one. Luckily it is not necessary nowadays to be a photographic expert in order to obtain a pleasant pictorial record of one's journeyings, but at the same time experience points many ways in which 100 per cent. efficiency may be more nearly approached. If you happen to have a real expert on board, I have nothing to say, of course; but otherwise I consider that the motorist's camera should be just as utterly simple as modern skill can make it. It should be instantly ready for use, since many of the incidents and scenes of which a snap is desired are evanescent, and while the photographer is fiddling with a complicated piece of apparatus the picture has ceased to exist.

Needless to say, the camera should be robust and almost impossible to put out of order, even with careless inexpert use; but in addition the lens should have more than the usual depth of focus, so that trivial errors of distance judgment do not result in a ruined film. The camera should be light and small, and of a convenient shape when closed to slip into coat or car pocket. The size of the picture taken is rather critical, I think. On the one hand it should not be so small that every negative needs enlargement before it is of any real interest, but on the other hand, too large a negative is wasteful of film and paper—or rather, of £ s. d.—since an enlargement can be cheaply and quickly obtained from each medium-sized film on which the picture is considered worthy of this treatment.

The film has come so generally into use that I suppose no motorist would even consider the possibility of taking plates on a tour, no matter how much he might prefer to use them at home. As between roll films and film packs, there is not a great deal to choose, except that in the latter case the removal of the exposed pack and the substitution of a fresh one is more quickly and easily performed. In price, weight, storage facility and so forth the advantages are similar; and against the superior facility of changing films of the pack type must be set the liability to fogging through careless handling or packing, from which the roll film does not suffer.

Unusual Views

In the course of my journeys, it has been necessary sometimes to snap scenes from the moving car in a fashion which the average motoring photographer would probably never dream of attempting, and I have an album of photographs taken through windscreen, side and rear windows which are surprisingly good, especially considering that both car and object photographed were often travelling at anything up to forty miles an hour. Particularly attractive are pictures taken from the rear compartment of the car, showing a clear silhouette of the driver at the wheel, with a view of the outside world seen through the windscreen in remarkably sharp definition. This may be freak photography, and I must admit that it does not come off every time, but it is an attempt well worth making.

So far as normal photography is concerned, it is probably advisable to carry a tripod, having first made sure that the camera has a bush into which the screw of the tripod fits, for in the course of an average tour there are almost certain to be some cathedral or cottage interiors that simply must be recorded, and of which the gloom necessitates a time exposure. Modern tubular tripods are both light and cheap, and they fold up into negligible space.

So many people know how to use a camera nowadays that I rather hesitate to give any really elementary hints. Presuming, however, that the motor tourist is a photographic novice, there is no reason why she should not obtain quite a large proportion of good results if a few simple rules are borne in mind. In the first place, the sun should be well over the shoulder of the operator. If it is directly ahead, and shining into the lens, a very poor photograph, if any, will result, while if it is directly behind, the shadow of the photographer herself will quite probably spoil the artistic composition of the picture.

Disappointing results which may be technically excellent are often obtained by beginners, and they wonder why the picture is so much less attractive than the actual scene. In nine cases out of ten, it is due to the fact that colour, or varied colours, were the actual making of the picture as seen with the eye, whereas, reduced to simple black and white, the scene is drab and uninteresting. Unless special precautions are taken, the lens has not the power of differentiating between the delicate shades which please the eye; and while it is a common saying that the camera cannot lie, it can certainly give a false rendering of colour. Red, for instance, is indistinguishable from black, and blue from white; and many a fascinating sunset or seascape which the ambitious novice has endeavoured to transfer to paper has failed for just that reason.

Another mistake that is easily made is an endeavour to include too much in a single negative. My opinions may be subject to criticism, but the simpler the subject, the more pleasing is the picture to my eye. Frequently, however, the snapshotter endeavours to take a picture that is too distant for the camera to deal with, the result being that the particular view required is reduced to pin-point dimensions, and is lost in a complicated mass of unwanted detail. Enlargement of the special bit that is required will often extract a picture from an apparent failure, it is true; but that is a cure, whereas prevention is so easily secured. Aim at simplicity; remember that form, rather than colour, is the making of a photographic negative; and *hold the camera steady!*

13

ON TAKING YOUR CAR ABROAD

A CONTINENTAL MOTOR tour would probably appeal to the majority of women motorists of small experience as an undertaking far beyond their powers, but as a matter of fact all the processes connected with the shipping of a car, and its introduction into foreign countries, are now so simplified that the difficulty is imaginary rather than real.

I am a deep believer in foreign touring, for several reasons. In the first place I think one appreciates one's own country much more fully from an experience of the conditions in other lands; and in the second the varied driving experience gained in three weeks or a month abroad is as good as a course of concentrated instruction. And, on top of all this, there is the novelty, the charm of fresh scenes.

But, as I say, many motorists are deterred by quite exaggerated ideas of the difficulties, and also of the cost. In regard to the latter, except for the freight across the Channel, I scarcely think it need be taken into account. Petrol, it is true, is usually slightly dearer than at home; but as hotel bills are very frequently considerably lower for similar accommodation the cost of a tour abroad is not strikingly different from that of one of the same mileage at home.

Before going any further, however, I ought to say quite definitely that foreign touring is practically impossible unless the traveller puts her affairs into the hands of one of the motoring organisations which is empowered to deal with customs matters and so on. The organisation arranges everything, charging only very moderate fees for the service, and the tourist leaves England with the pleasant knowledge that all that there might have been of complication has been straightened out in advance.

As can be imagined, a tour covering more than one foreign country, with different customs duties in force, would present serious financial problems if no special measures were in force. But by virtue of the activities of our organisations, a uniform deposit of £50 in cash has been arranged for, to cover the temporary importation of any car into any country (of those which have entered into the agreement). This the tourist has to find, but as it is only a deposit, returnable when the car re-enters England, it is not a very serious matter. In addition, however, a banker's guarantee for the balance of the highest customs duty levied in any of the countries on the tourist's itinerary must be furnished; or, failing this, it is possible to take out an insurance policy for a moderate premium against the possibility that the payment of this balance will be necessary. This possibility arises only if the owner chooses to dispose of her car abroad, in which case of course the ordinary import duty in force in that particular country becomes payable.

Transporting the Car

In the matter of shipping the car to the Continent, a little discretion should be used. On all the cross-Channel routes, wheelbase is the basis of charge. Dover–Calais and Folkestone–Boulogne prices are identical throughout the range; but Newhaven–Dieppe, while the same as the other two for the smaller types of car, is considerably cheaper for cars of more than 9 ft. 6 ins. wheelbase. On the other hand, Southampton–Havre and Southampton–St. Malo are the most expensive routes for small cars, but come between the scales of the other crossings for larger vehicles. I will give a complete list of the charges ruling at the time of writing, so that the intending tourist can figure things out for herself, in relation to the particular car which she possesses.

WHEELBASE	DOVER–CALAIS & FOLKESTONE– BOULOGNE	NEWHAVEN– DIEPPE	SOUTHAMPTON–HAVRE & SOUTHAMPTON– ST. MALO
up to 8 ft 6 ins	£3 15 0	£3 15 0	£4 0 0
up to 9 ft 0 ins	£4 15 0	£4 15 0	£5 0 0
up to 9 ft 6 ins	£6 10 0	£6 10 0	£6 15 0
up to 10 ft 6 ins	£8 10 0	£7 10 0	£7 15 0
over 10 ft 6 ins	£10 0 0	£8 10 0	£8 15 0

All these figures, it should be pointed out, are the charges at owner's risk. Cars may be sent by any of these routes at company's risk at a higher cost, varying from about twenty-five shillings on the smallest cars to over £3 extra on the largest. If owner's risk is chosen, marine insurance can be effected at a few shillings per cent.

For those who prefer to travel via the Dover–Ostend route, I will give the following details:

WHEELBASE	CLOSED CAR	TOURER
up to 7 ft 6 ins	£2 18 10	£2 18 10
up to 8 ft 6 ins	£3 10 8	£3 4 3
up to 9 ft 6 ins	£4 2 5	£3 16 3
up to 9 ft 6 ins	£4 14 2	£4 2 5
up to 10 ft 6 ins	£5 5 11	£4 7 1
up to 10 ft 6 ins	£5 17 8	£4 11 3
up to 13 ft 1 in	£6 9 5	£5 5 11

In the case of Dover–Ostend, cars cannot be shipped at company's risk, but they can, of course, be insured. The actual cost of insurance on this and all the other cross-Channel routes except Southampton–St. Malo, which is very slightly higher, is half-a-crown per cent. for ordinary risks and three-and-six to include risk against floating mines, for the single journey. Return journey insurance rates are exactly double.

Various other more or less trivial charges are made, notably landing and embarkation dues, and agent's fees, at the Continental ports, but as a sovereign will more than cover them in most cases, it is not worth going into details here. The agent's fee, in any case, is money very well spent, for he meets the traveller on arrival at the foreign port, relieves her of her papers, attends to all formalities, arranges for the refilling of the petrol—now *essence*—tank, and merely asks her to sign the various documents. The whole process of disembarking the car, completing the formalities, and getting out on to the open road is completed without worry or delay, and I am quite sure that once the first experience of foreign touring is over, it will be oft repeated.

Information on such points as the time of sailing, and the exact time in advance at which the shipping company requires the car to be alongside ready for embarkation will be furnished by the motoring organisation through which one deals; but generally speaking the car should be at the quayside about two hours before sailing time.

While the majority of women motorists will not wish to go farther afield than France and Belgium, especially on a first tour, it is worth while considering the possibility, in the future, if not at once, of the glorious North African coast as a touring ground. Splendid roads, ultra luxurious hotels and complete novelty await the visitor. The roads of Morocco, and the unspoilt mediævalism of Fez and Marrakesh alone are worth the extra trouble of reaching them, while Tunisia and Algeria have their individual attractions. Unless time is no object, it is probably better, as well as cheaper, to ship all the way to Algeria, rather than to travel partly overland. The rates are extremely reasonable, considering the distance; £15, plus two guineas dock dues, are charged for a car not exceeding 24 cwt., and £20 plus three guineas for heavier vehicles.

Going North

So far as Northern Europe is concerned, it is possible to ship direct to various North Sea and Baltic ports, but roads are so good and interest is so varied that I should distinctly advise the overland route to Denmark and Scandinavia generally. Copenhagen can be reached by way of Ostend, Antwerp, Nijmegen, Osnabrück, Bremen and Hamburg in less than a week with comfort. I have done Ostend to Copenhagen in three days without too great a strain, though that, naturally, left no time for sightseeing. After passing out of the still debatable districts of Schleswig-Holstein, Denmark reveals itself as a perfect little gem of a country; while a further day's journey across the Sound from Hälsingör (the Elsinore of Hamlet) to Hälsingborg in Sweden opens up to the tourist a veritable fairyland of lake and forest scenery, with, if season is right and time available, the attraction of the Midnight Sun to lead one ever farther northward. In no countries have I found a heartier welcome for British visitors than in these lands of the North; nor in any country better fare, cleaner, fresher atmosphere, or greater charm.

But there, the woman motor tourist has infinite variety from which to choose; and from it all she will almost inevitably select France and the attractive highway South to the Riviera for her first venture abroad.

14

DRIVING HINTS FOR CONTINENTAL TOURISTS

IMAGINED DIFFICULTIES with languages and differing rules of the road are probably the principal deterrents to more general foreign touring, but really very little trouble is experienced in regard to either matter. As to the language, it is obviously possible for one person to have only a bare nodding acquaintance with more than a very few of the tongues and dialects encountered in Continental ramblings, and it is astonishing how far English, plus half-remembered schoolgirl French will carry one. As a golden rule, I should say try your English first. Almost invariably, in garage or hotel, someone within earshot will understand it, and will very readily come to your assistance.

The rule of the road is a little different, for, from the moment of landing on foreign soil the tourist has to reverse all her usual driving habits. Curiously enough, it has been not only my own experience, but that of nearly everyone whom I have consulted on the subject, that the real difficulty is not of getting into the way of keeping to the right and overtaking on the left, but of re-adopting the English rule of the road on returning home. For some reason which I cannot explain, driving on the right seems to come natural to the majority of people right from the start, and the only danger to be feared is that when, after driving over deserted roads for some time, another car approaches, the instinct to draw over to the left to leave it room to pass may momentarily prove too strong. The mere fact that the other driver, provided that he is a native, holds his ground forces you to remember in plenty of time to avoid any real trouble, but this is certainly a point to be guarded against just for the first day on foreign ground. Keep telling yourself: "Drive on the right!" Instruct your passengers to shout it at you when occasion arises—just for the first day. After that there will be no need.

There are other points which are more difficult to get used to, and particularly in Paris you must adopt the methods of the local drivers if you want peace. They drive almost entirely on their funny little squeaky hooters, and "peep-peep" their way across all crossings without slackening speed. It is almost essential, in fact, to invest in a similar horn before crossing the Channel, as raucous electric horns must not be used in towns, while the more dignified variety of those which we use at home seem to carry no weight whatever. And, having purchased a squeaky hooter, peep-peep for all you're worth at every cross road and round every corner!

On the wonderful, straight *routes nationales*, all is plain sailing, but down the Riviera, with the interminable hairpin bends of the Corniche and mountain roads, a great deal of caution is required. Keep in as close as you can, not forgetting the hooter, round every bend, and avoid taking risks.

Other Times, Other Manners

Different countries have different peculiarities in regard to driving habits. On a first trip across Holland and Germany, for instance, one is apt to be embarrassed by the apparent determination of the many cyclists to disregard the rule of the road altogether. They come flocking towards you indiscriminately on either side, the reason being that quite frequently special tracks exist alongside the motor road for their use. Among themselves they seem to have no rule, and as the cars do not encroach on the cycle tracks, they are safe enough. When the presence of this track is obvious, the motoring stranger is not so much at a loss; but the cyclists act on the same principle whether there is an actual track or not!

For the most part the visitor will avoid night travel as much as possible, but it is worth while remembering that the use of headlamps is not permitted in French towns, and even on the open road, French motorists are most scrupulous in observing the lighting regulations. These provide that you must dim or extinguish your headlamps to avoid dazzle on meeting another car. There is no choice in the matter in France, and the difference from our haphazard conditions is a little startling just at first. The difficulty here is that for many kilometres on end the main roads are dead straight, and often it is necessary to run on sidelamps only for the greater part of the time, since approaching lamps can be seen from so far away. The obvious solution of the difficulty is the use of a spotlight which can be readily switched on, or, better still, which automatically comes into action when the head-lamps are switched off. If this is trained on the right hand edge of the road at a distance ahead which best suits the speed of the car and the focus of the driver's eyes, no inconvenience is felt from the French lighting regulations.

Another point to bear in mind is that while there is no speed limit on the open country roads of France, every village has its very much reduced limit, and it is advisable to make at least a show of observing the limit. The police let you severely alone so long as you do no harm, but I understand that if an accident is caused through driving, one is placed in a very difficult position, the lack of facility with the French language being a serious disadvantage.

A first visit abroad is an education in what can be done in the way of signposting and road signs generally, and in regard to the latter it is advisable always to pay close attention to their warnings. When a bump is indicated, at a stated distance ahead, it *is* a bump; one that may easily break a spring if you have been inattentive. The beauty of these signs, however, is that they call for practically no knowledge of French, being strictly and very graphically pictorial. Direction indications are placed in such positions, and given in letters and figures so large that they can be read without slackening speed, while even in towns and villages the walls of cottages are so inscribed that the stranger need never be in doubt of her way.

So far as traffic driving on the Continent generally is concerned, there is no more difficulty than at home, for even in Paris the reputed recklessness and slap-dash methods of the taximen has been checked by sheer weight of numbers. The one-way street and gyratory traffic systems are much more general in France; and I may say that close attention to the rules is required, since the police will positively never let you get away with a mistake.

There is not much more one need say with regard to foreign touring. As mentioned before, most of the difficulties are imaginary. See your own country first, by all means. But a trip abroad undoubtedly enables one to give keener appreciation to the advantages of our own land, besides pointing ways in which conditions at home could be improved.